Lily, Sam & Bertie

For all those impacted by MND

by Andy & Victoria Stonehouse

Uncle Sam and Aunty Emma brought home a puppy,
A little friend to make them smile.

Bertie was a Cocker Spaniel,

Who jumped about all the while.

Sam helped Bertie, and Bertie helped Sam,

But Lily was scared of dogs, she wasn't Bertie's biggest fan.

"He'll chase me,

bark at me,

bite me and then,

He'll chase me, bark at me and bite me again!"

"Not Bertie!" Said Emma, "Not Bertie!" Said Sam,
"He's as good as gold, he's our clever little man."

"Do you want to help teach him Lily?" Aunty Emma asked,

"Bertie likes earning treats when we give him little tasks."

Lily wasn't sure this would to be fun to do,
She started to get nervous and backed away in fear.

She thought he was the cutest thing ever,
But didn't want him anyway near.

"Let's try something simple" suggested Uncle Sam,

"Stay!" Sam said to Bertie and he sat very still.

Aunty Emma put a treat in the palm of her hand,
Lily was worried but Bertie didn't move at all.

"Good boy!" said Uncle Sam, And Bertie slowly stood.

He walked and wagged his way to Aunty Emma,
And took the biscuit when she said he could.

"Woah!" Said Lily,
"See!" Said Uncle Sam.

Bertie was as good as gold,
Their clever little man.

"Do you want to help this time?"
Lily wasn't sure.

The last time she'd met a dog,

It jumped up with muddy paws!

"Place treats in these boxes" Sam said with a smile,
Lily put them in, Bertie wagged his tail all the while.

"Stand back and watch him" Uncle Sam declared,
Bertie found every treat, while Lily stood and stared.

"Amazing!" Said Lily, "See!" Said Sam.

Bertie was as good as gold,
Their clever little man.

Mia the cat didn't trust Bertie at all.
This little puppy was trouble for sure.

She didn't want Lily upset again
So she showed Bertie the door.

"Where's Bertie gone now?" said Lily,

"I'm not sure" said Uncle Sam.

They set off to look for him, where could he be?

They had to find their clever little man.

They searched up and down

and all around,

Lily looked under the bed and Bertie was found.

"He's stuck!" cried Lily with a shout,
She crawled under the bed and gently pulled Bertie out.

She hugged and squeezed little Bertie,
Lily was relieved he was safe and sound.

From that moment on they were the best of friends,
All of them were delighted little Bertie had been found.

"Do you feel better Lily?" asked Uncle Sam
"I do" Lily said, "I'm not scared of Bertie any more."

"Good" said Uncle Sam, "you looked out for him,

And that's what best friends are for."

Sam Perkins is the brother of the authors of the 'Adventures of Lily' Books. At the age of 37, he was diagnosed with Motor Neurone Disease and reacted by starting his own charity, Stand Against MND (SAM).

SAM raises money to fund research towards a cure and treatments for MND and also funds palliative care for those affected by MND. All profits from the sales of this book will be donated to Stand Against MND.

If you would like to know more about SAM please follow
@standagainstMND on Facebook, Instagram and Twitter.

If Sam has inspired you and you would like to join TeamSAM to help fundraise, you can contact the charity via the social media channels above or email **standagainstmnd@gmail.com**

Lily, Sam & Bertie

First published 2021 by Moosehead Publishing
This edition published 2021 by Moosehead Publishing

ISBN: 978-1-9161804-6-8

Text copyright © Andy Stonehouse & Victoria Stonehouse 2021

Illustrations copyright © Andy Stonehouse 2021

A CIP catalogue record of this book is available from the British Library

Also in the series:

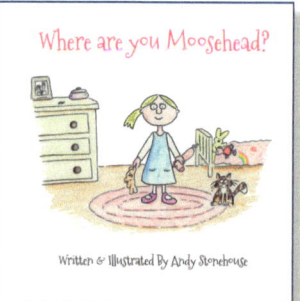

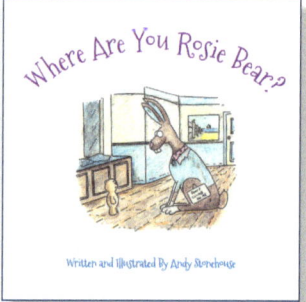

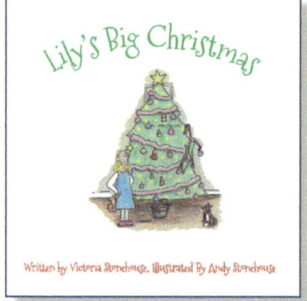

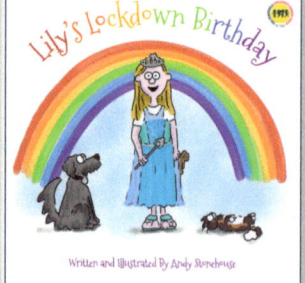

www.adventuresoflily.com

www.ingramcontent.com/pod-product-compliance
Lightning Source LLC
Chambersburg PA
CBHW041003170626
46815CB00002B/132